One Life Changes Everything

By

Lorelei R. Jensen

To Betsy,

Without you overhyping me, I don't think I would have had the courage to write. We will always be friends because you know far too much. I wish you the best in the world

Chapter 1

Death is an equalizer.

As he sat by his grandfather's bedside, Joshua couldn't shake out that thought. "Death is an equalizer." No one can escape it. It will come for the young, the old, the rich, the poor. No matter how good or bad you are, death will come for you. There is no escape. One may avoid it for a time, but its dark hands will drag you down eventually. No hope can arise from the inevitable darkness death causes.

His grandfather was a lucky fellow, able to escape death's grasp for now. With his artery now replaced, he would go home sooner rather than later. Unlike others in this hospital who only had mere moments left in their dismal lives, his grandfather got to go home and be with a happy family who wasn't ready for him to go.

Joshua's phone vibrated. He let himself out of his grandfather's room, answering the call as he closed the door. He barely listened to his mother's exasperating shrieking, trying to find a place to escape the beeping of the machinery and the murmuring of the nurses, patients, and visitors. She scolded his rude and horrible behavior for not visiting his grouchy, ungrateful grandfather. The nurses walked around him. Little did his mother know, he had gone without telling her. He was already an adult. Why did she find the need to berate him about everything?

"I get it," he growled. "Just chill. I'm already visiting Grandpa, so you don't need to nag."

His mom sighed. Joshua hung up before she could rail on him for being a horrible child and not turning out how she expected. What did she expect? It's not like she'd been doing much in his life. She rarely sent money anymore, despite knowing that he couldn't pay for his rent and tuition. Spinning on his heels, he headed towards his grandfather's room. Or so he thought. He swore. The two rooms side by side were identical and he couldn't remember which one was his grandfather's. Why didn't they put the names on the door?

He ran his hand through his short black hair, slid open the door on the left, and walked in, hoping it was the right one. As soon as he shut the door, he knew it was wrong. A little girl, about eight years old, sat on the bed. Her blue eyes, like the ocean on a clear day, brightened when she saw him. Joshua tried to back out, but the little girl hopped off her bed and practically skipped over to him. A pink beanie covered her head. She was gaunt and pale.

She hugged his leg. "Did Mama ask you to play with me?" She grinned. "I'm so happy."

"No, actually…"

"Here, you can play with my bunny." She tugged on his arm and dragged him after her. She sat on her bed after forcing him into the chair next to her. "My name is Alice, but Mama calls me Allie. What's your name?"

Joshua tried to smile, but he was too irritated. "I'm Joshua." When would her parents get back? He had plans and needed to leave in the next half an hour or he'd be late.

She gave him a grin that showed her missing front teeth. She pushed a once fluffy pink bunny into his hand. It needed a good washing as dirt was matted deep into the fluff. In her hands, she held a ratty lion that had probably been yellow at one point in its life but was now brown. She held it to her chest like it was the most precious thing in the world.

"Josh, you dress funny." She giggled. "Why do your pants have holes in them?"

He rolled his eyes. Alice sang in a high-pitched and squeaky voice as she made her lion dance. She looked up at him and pouted.

"You too." she demanded.

He glared at her. "What?"

"Make Bunny dance too."

Josh sighed before making the bunny twirl around. Alice burst into laughter. Her beanie slid off a bit, revealing her lack of hair. There was a huge bruise forming on her wrist.

"That's not how you do it. Watch." She grabbed the lion's waist and made it do a floppy dance. She deepened her voice and made weird talking noises. Without looking, she grabbed her bunny and talked in an even higher-pitched voice about how wonderful the ball was going.

Josh thought of excuses to give so he could leave as Alice played by herself.

"I'm so happy Mama sent you. It's boring being here by myself. The nurses can't play with me." She held her toys to her chest. "Let's go on a walk."

Alice got off her bed. She clasped onto Joshua's hand. He couldn't understand her little mind. She excitedly dragged him out of the room. Her blue eyes turned to him. He figured that she shouldn't get up from her bed, which was fine with him. Joshua just wanted to leave.

He hated children. They were whining and annoying. Snot always dripped from their noses. They tended to be dirty. And just like this brat, they demanded their will and way.

"Can you carry me? Mama says I shouldn't walk too much."

Josh looked around for a nurse to do it, but they were running around. Something must have happened. With great annoyance, he picked her up. She was frail and tiny. Skinny arms wrapped tightly around his neck. He shivered. His nose wrinkled from the heavy smell of antiseptics.

"Yay! Let's go."

He followed her pointing. She introduced all the patients as they passed by their doors. She mentioned their weight and hair loss a ton. Josh walked Alice all over the floor until they were in front of those two doors. She pointed to the one which he had finally learned was his grandfather's. Wiggling out of his arms, Alice pushed open the door. She trotted in like she owned the place.

"Papa, I made a friend today," she squealed.

"Oh, really?" His gruff voice was soft. "Who might it be?"

His grandfather smiled, which caused Josh a great deal of shock. The old man opened his arms, and Alice practically shot into them. His grandfather cradled the child in his arms. Their grey eyes locked and his grandfather raised an eyebrow. Alice chattered for fifteen minutes before coughing. Each wet cough shook her body. Her eyes drooped and she fought a yawn.

Josh made himself comfortable in the chair next to the bed. He played on his phone, ignoring the three missed calls from his mom. His ex-girlfriend had sent him a pity message as well. He blocked her number and felt more cross than before he had come. There was another girl anyway who was more beautiful and kind. Plus, her figure was amazing.

"Mr. Holdem, it's time for your— Alice, why are you in here? You've already taken three walks today," a large African-American nurse with muscles that could burst watermelons said. He cheerfully picked up Alice.

"I was introducing Josh to everyone." Alice laughed. "Mr. Polis, is Mama going to visit me today?"

The nurse cringed. "Maybe."

"I hope so." She leaned into Mr. Polis's shoulder. "I miss her a lot."

He soothed her and rubbed her back. Whistling, he took her back to her own room with a promise to come back with Josh's grandfather's medicine.

"So you entered the wrong room?" Grandfather asked with a small chuckle. His stormy eyes calmed.

"I tried to escape."

"She just pulls everyone along, doesn't she?"

Josh leaned his head back. Exhaustion rolled over him. "She talks so much. Why do kids talk so much?"

His grandfather shook his head. "I'm glad you stayed with her. Her mother is trying to come, but it's hard financially and emotionally."

Josh pitied the kid. She must have felt abandoned by her parents, not knowing when they were coming by or if they would come at all. He understood that lonely and constricting feeling. Something that still bothered him as an adult.

He never wanted to interact with that child again. It took too much out of him.

"You should visit her tomorrow as well. It would make the child's day," his grandfather said. "She doesn't have many days left to enjoy."

Nurse Polis walked in. "It would. Her mother just called and said she couldn't come by today either. I heard she is saving her paid time off so she can spend a couple of weeks with her."

Josh's grandfather nodded solemnly and a gloomy quiet that Josh couldn't fully understand filled the room. Mr. Polis gave his grandfather his medicine.

"You'll be free to go in a couple of days." Mr. Polis smiled at his grandpa. "Just keep taking care of yourself."

Josh told everyone goodbye before heading out. Hopefully, he wouldn't come back to the hospital. After all, he only did it to appease his nagging old hag. Plus, seeing a dying child wasn't on the top of his list of things he wanted to do.

Chapter 2

Josh rested his head on a pretty shoulder. Beer spilled on the table as his buddies messed around. A girl ran gentle, teasing fingers in his soft hair. His head spun, but he still found her soft lips. She giggled before pulling him closer. One of his friends pushed him towards her. She crawled into his lap. The loud music of the bar pounded against his brain and he fought the urge to vomit.

Eric, his friend, made out with some girl across the table. They stood up, falling over each other. People laughed as the two stumbled around. His girl slapped him on the rear as they went to one of their houses.

"Want to leave?" Josh asked. He let his hands follow the curve of her hips. She nodded excitedly. At least that's what he thought she did. His head was so foggy that he honestly couldn't tell.

She pulled him up. He leaned against her as they walked to his car. She smelled like sunflowers with a hint of cigarette. Not his favorite smell, but it wasn't like they'd remember each other in the morning.

Josh drove home. It wasn't the best idea as he ran two lights and had to swerve out of the way for a person. Ballads ran throughout the car. His mind was heavy and fuzzy. After that night, Josh couldn't remember getting home.

He was up throughout the whole night. At first as always, his heart pitter-pattered with excitement, but while the night went on everything died down. The fun turned into empty heartache. Even as she whispered words of love into his ear, as she pressed her lips against his neck, the moment turned into empty actions. There was a ravishing feeling in his heart, wanting more and more of something, anything. The more girls he slept with, the more alcohol he drank, as he fed his heart the licentiousness of life, he craved more.

The girl left before he woke, though he wasn't surprised. His sheets were crumpled underneath him. Josh buried his face into his pillow. He sighed before getting up. The emptiness from the night took over his mind and the craving of something more created an uncomfortable ache in his soul. A ringing sounded across the room.

"Mom," he sleepily mumbled into the speaker.

Her high pitched voice shot through his hangover. "Don't tell me you brought another girl over. I didn't raise you to be this way. What if you get a disease?"

Josh groaned. How did she know? "What do you want?" He picked up his shirt from the floor, sniffed it, and put it back. It was time to do laundry. The monstrous pile of laundry made its way into the hall and crawled into the living room.

"I'm cutting off our money for you. You need to get a grip on your life before we're willing to help out."

Anger flashed through him. "What's wrong with my life? I can do whatever I want."

"We know, but your father and I cannot condone your behavior so we made our decision. You need to make yours." Her voice sounded sad like tears were about to fall. Josh didn't believe her acting though. She must've hated him and wanted to cut ties to see him suffer.

He hung up and threw the phone against the wall. The screen shattered. Glass sunk into his skin as he picked it back up. Squatting, Josh cursed and left the mess so he could take a shower.

The hot water washed away his anger, but left an ache. The sleepiness wore off and brought out his unpleasant feelings. Josh let the water run down his back. Soap dripped into his eye and it watered, blending into the stream. The aching in his chest made him want a drink, something to ease his mind.

Maybe, he'd call out sick. Josh determined otherwise. His parents weren't going to help, so he needed to make as much money as possible. Work would distract him. The feelings of betrayal raged through his veins. With residual anger lingering, Josh readied for work.

Chapter 3

Alice held her stuffed lion close to her chest as pain dully throbbed everywhere. A slight breeze danced across her room. Spring flowers sat on the windowsill. They brightened up the bland white interior. She carefully padded to the window, struggling to drag her equipment next to her. With each step, her legs shook.

Her eyes wandered across the small town. Behind her hometown, mountains rose high into the sky, touching clouds with their rugged tops. Rich blues and yellows graced the sky. She happily watched cars drive down the asphalt roads. To her, everything was beautiful: the people, the landscape, the smells, even when she didn't look beautiful.

The door opened behind her. Mama shuffled into the room. Mama gasped and carried Alice back to her bed.

Blankets piled on top of her, and Mama gently tucked them around Alice's tiny body.

"You shouldn't get up, Treasure. You could injure yourself or what if you have an attack." Mama brushed her hand through her thick brown curls.

Alice began to argue back, but a glare from her mama shut her up quickly. A phone call took her mama away again. Mama was always gone. Alice tried not to be upset, but she wanted her to stay, stay by her side before she died.

Alice knew she would die. Sometimes, reality hit harder than anyone could understand. They acted like she was five, not understanding that time was running out, but she knew every day that her life was slipping away. Away and away, each time she closed her eyes, it became harder to bear. She didn't want to be alone anymore.

Mama walked back in and the solemn, controlling mood had fled. Alice relished in Mama's presence. Even when she was gone, Mama would remember her. When she was home with Jesus, Mama would still be loving.

Alice pasted on her most cheerful smile. It brought out dimples on her cheek, though her weight loss got rid of most of her dimple. The cheeriness made Mama grin back. Mama didn't know about Alice's fear and sadness. Mama was already so sad. After Daddy died, Mama couldn't handle too much. It saddened Alice to see Mama cry.

"I wish you could have met Josh," Alice explained. "He's just like Daddy before he met Jesus."

Mama shook her head. "You never met Daddy before he met Jesus."

Alice giggled. "But you told me that he was like a puppy looking for its mommy."

"I did, didn't I?"

"Were you talking to Mr. Fiskar?"

Mama beamed. She smiled more since dating Mr. Fiskar and once Alice was gone they'd get married. Mama said that wasn't the case, but Alice knew better. Only a few months earlier, Mama barely smiled. She worked all day and slept all night. Some weeks, getting her to go to church was a miracle. Mr. Fiskar was nice, but Alice liked Daddy way more.

"I'm very glad that Jesus sent you a friend. Mama knows you've been praying for one." Mama kissed Alice's forehead. "I've got to go to work, but I'll be back tomorrow."

Alice stared out the window. A glowing light caught her attention. Though she saw nothing, something had to have passed the window.

"I wonder if Josh'll come back," Alice whispered when she was by herself.

Chapter 4

Joshua grumbled as he stalked into his grandfather's room. Only a few days had passed since his last visit. The plan to avoid going to the hospital crashed and burned when he couldn't find his college textbook. Class was tomorrow and he still hadn't finished his assignment. There was only one place he could have left it.

Nurses greeted him with a smile as they passed him. With an irritated reluctancy, Joshua knocked on the door. He entered despite not hearing an answer. His grandfather laid on the bed. His attention never left the T.V.

"It's on the chair," the old man said in a grumpy growl. "Go visit Alice while you're here. Her mom needs to talk to the doctor."

Joshua sighed, grabbed his textbook, and headed over to Alice's room. This time he waited for a response before entering. A slight breeze flowed through the room. Despite being a hospital room, the stench of antiseptics was not overwhelming. Instead, a flowery scent tickled his nose.

"Josh!" Alice sat up in her bed. A breathing tube rested under her nose and an IV hung from her elbow. A halo of light bounced off her golden beanie. She looked like those naked baby angel things. A cherub, if Josh remembered correctly. There was no meat on her bones. She was weaker than his last visit. The bags under her eyes carved into her face.

By her side, holding two dolls, sat an older woman with salt-and-pepper hair. She turned her deep, sorrowful blue eyes towards him. Exhaustion lined her face.

"I'm Marie Casablanca, Alice's mom," she said. Even her voice was lined with exhaustion. She offered her hand. Her cuticles bled from over chewing.

Shaking it, Joshua spoke, "Joshua Willoughberg. My grandfather is in the next room." He leaned forward to whisper. "He said you needed to talk to the doctor. I'll hang out with her while you do."

Her shoulders sagged and tears welled in her eyes. "Oh, thank you so much." Marie kissed Alices' forehead. "I will be right back, Love. Be good while Mama's gone."

"Okay." Alice grabbed her dolls from her mom.

Marie patted Josh's hand gratefully. "You are a blessing."

Marie hurriedly walked out. Joshua snatched her seat beside the bed. He hated pretending to be nice. Not only was he bored out of his wits, but taking care of little kids killed him. He pasted on a smile. Alice gave him an odd look before breaking into chatter.

"It's only been a couple of days and you've turned into a robot." Josh jokingly scolded.

Machines strapped onto her and an IV pierced her skin. Despite her obvious discomfort, she beamed like nothing was wrong. At her age, she should know that she was dying. Most kids bawled and laid depressed all day. Why did this child not react to her death?

As if she could read his mind, she said, "I'm gonna meet Jesus soon."

"Jesus, huh?" Joshua let sarcasm encase each word.

Alice nodded excitedly. "Daddy's gonna be there too. It'll be tons of fun." She paused. A solemn look, not suited for a child that young, crossed her face. "Mama's going to be all alone though. But I know God will take care of her. He'll make sure she doesn't get too lonely."

Josh slowly nodded. He knew there was no god.
No afterlife. Heaven and Hell were places created to
manipulate people so that they didn't behave badly. Even
if there was a "god," it's not like he cared. Why would
bad things happen if he loves humans? She won't even be
disappointed when she dies since her soul was just going
to oblivion. Too bad she'd been lied to her whole life.

He tuned out her incessant chatter. He turned to
his phone. Amy finally texted him back. Finally,
something good. She was the most beautiful girl he'd ever
seen and she kept inviting him out. He'd been hanging out
with her off and on for weeks. Last night, Josh gathered
up the courage and asked her out.

The response startled him. He thought they were
getting along, but the text proved otherwise. She swore at
him and called him gross and disgusting. "How dare he
ask her out" and other such things. Joshua's spirit fell.

They'd been out to coffee and dinner before. In their

conversations, he had been careful with what he said. He

could've sworn she liked him back.

"Josh." Alice tugged on his sleeve. Worry creased

her little brow. "You ok?"

He fumbled for his words. "Not really. The girl I

liked is actually a bi— I mean a nasty person." Why was

he admitting this to a little girl? She couldn't even

comprehend what he was feeling. Also, why was she so

nosy? Little children.

She placed her hands on her thin waist. With

gusto, she shouted, "That's no good. I know the cure

though." Her confidence induced a small chuckle from

him.

Joshua smirked. "And?"

Alice grabbed his hands and bowed her head.

"Dear Heavenly Father, Lord, thank you for this day.

Please help Josh. He's not doing too good. Thank you for

sending Jesus to die for our sins. I love you and can't wait to see you. In Jesus name, Amen." She lifted her head and grinned like a kid on Christmas. "Now, we watch a movie."

Josh didn't know how he felt praying to a god who didn't exist, but whatever floats her boat. Hopefully, she didn't put on those weird Christian vegetable movies. He didn't know if he'd be able to handle singing and dancing veggies.

"We even have Netflix. Sit next to me." She patted her bed excitedly.

He sighed. "Fine. Make room."

Alice moved her cords and tubes, letting him sit beside her. She handed him the remote and he scrolled through the selection. Finally, after much pestering, he picked *The Bee Movie*. It was funnier than it should've been for a twenty-three year old. All the politics didn't ruin the humor. He expected Marie to come back, but the movie finished and she still wasn't back. Alice slept on his side, her sickness getting the best of her. She sucked on the arm of her lion. It dripped with saliva. Josh inwardly squirmed.

The warm afternoon light floated on his skin, while a slight breeze brushed through his hair. Birds chirped their songs outside the window. Alice snuggled into his side. In the back of his mind, his need to finish his homework nagged him, sounding somewhat like his mother. Even, the rude awakening from that girl that had overwhelmed him before dimmed into a slight ache. Without even realizing, he nodded off.

* * *

Someone shook Joshua. He sat up, panicked. The window was closed and no sunlight crossed the sky. "Mr. Willoughberg, visitor hours are about to end." Marie's voice was watery and thick. "You should probably go. Thank you for staying with my Treasure."

Alice was conked out next to him. Her hand clung onto his shirt. "Allie, let go," he said half-heartedly.

She did as he asked and turned to her side. He didn't think she was actually awake. The oxygen fwished in her nose. Cautiously, he scooted off the bed. Rubbing the sleep out of his eyes, he tried to compose himself. Marie's face was red and puffy. She clenched her hands together. She held them so hard that they were turning white.

"Are you alright?" he asked.

She patted her eyes with a soppy tissue. "I'm— I'm." She wailed as if her heart was being broken.

He wrapped his arm around her shoulder. Alice shifted in her sleep. Josh paled. "Why don't we talk outside?"

The nurse, Polis, met them at the door. His face was grim. The hallway was colder than Josh remembered it being and it was one hundred percent quieter than it had been in the afternoon. The lights were dimmed and the air was still around them.

"I just don't know what to do." Marie buried her head into her hands. "I don't even have Alex around. I wonder why God is punishing me like this."

Nurse Polis sighed. "You know that isn't the case, Marie," he scolded. "There could be a reason besides punishment. She might be this way for someone other than you." Nurse Polis gaze landed on Josh.

Marie followed his gaze and they both stared at him for a moment. "You're definitely right." She dried her eyes and nodded. "I'm sorry. I just— I just don't know what to do. She's all I have left."

Josh felt a little uncomfortable. People kept dragging him into a fantasy. He couldn't believe a nurse who had seen the world at its worst could believe in a god.

She grabbed his arm, eyes pleading. "Will you please come tomorrow? Alice could really use a friend. To tell you the truth, she had been praying for someone to visit her. Maybe, you're the answer to that prayer."

Josh began to protest, but they never left his mouth. The poor child sitting by herself in the hospital room pulled on heart strings he didn't know he had. With a last look at the room, his excuses died completely. "I can make some time to visit."

Chapter 5

His house looked as though it had been ransacked. Dirty and clean clothes hung on every surface or were piled on the floor. Stacks of dirty dishes made their way out of the sink. A side table was knocked over from an angry stupor. Rotting food and bad hygiene clashed with the sterile scent of the hospital Josh had gotten used to. Food and drink were crusted into the carpet and the fan had a year's worth of dust piled onto it.

He kicked empty beer bottles away from the saggy couch. An old pizza box lay next to his laptop. Josh gagged. The smell was way worse up close. Pulling the laptop away from the cluttered table, he escaped into his equally messy bedroom. For a moment, he considered grabbing a beer, but decided finishing his essay would be easier if he didn't get drunk. His self control could be lacking.

His phone vibrated on his pillow. "What do you want, Eric?"

"I called you three times. Brandon broke his arm and is staying with his parents." Each word slurred into the next. "Where you've been? I looked around for ya. I thought ya finally left town, escaped your ma and all."

"I've been at the hospital."

There was a long pause before Eric snored. What did Joshua expect? Knowing Eric, he was probably drunk at some girl's house. Josh hung up and sighed.

The assignment took little time to complete and he considered going straight to bed. He stepped on a plate of old food, and his lip curled in disgust. The hospital had been so clean, and cold, that he forgot how disgusting his own home was. There was no way he could continue visiting Alice if his house was like this. What if he brought some sort of bacteria or germ and made her even more sick? He shivered. What if he's the reason she'd die?

Josh gathered the dirty dishes with a new found sense of cleanliness. He cleaned deep into the night. He scrubbed the floors and dishes, picked up the laundry, and sorted it so it could be washed. The carpet needed to be removed. There were puke stains so deep, he couldn't imagine how they would come out.

He stumbled into class the next morning. He nodded off a couple of times, but he felt way better than he had two days ago. Cleaning was strangely therapeutic. Though he had no plans of letting his house get that bad ever again.

* * *

Josh ran into class. His head pounded. The night had been a long one. He finally cleaned the toilet after who knows how long. He scrubbed his bathroom spotless. He regretted staying up late as he scooted into his desk.

"You shoulda been there last night." Eric slurred all his words. He was as high as a kite. Usually, Josh would've laughed, but his exhaustion, and something else, found Eric's behavior disgusting.

Amy ran up beside him. A hickey formed on her neck. She draped her body on top of Eric's. Josh wasn't jealous, only disappointed. All of his emotions that were once fiery and explosive had dulled. Everything was beginning to feel different. Girls, booze, parties, they all seemed to fade into the distance. For the first time, he realized how unhappy he was. Unhappy with his life, with his relationships, and most of all, he was upset at who he was.

Eric smelled heavily like pot. Josh gagged and scooted back. His face crinkled in disgust as Eric stepped closer.

Eric growled. "You have a problem?"

"Yes, actually, could you back off? You smell like crap and you're as drunk as a sailor."

Eric had always been very hostile. His fist slammed into Josh's face before he could comprehend what was happening. Eric's face was as red as a tomato. Amy jumped back in shock. Josh stood up as Eric stumbled angrily towards him. His cheeks puffed out.

The professor started the lesson despite Eric's language and violence. His American history lesson consisted of the Civil Rights Movement. Josh left before he was completely demolished. Eric ran after him. Josh was faster. His head throbbed horribly and his nausea came back full force.

A security guard caught Eric as Josh rounded a corner. He slowed to a walk and rubbed his forehead. Sweat dripped from his brows and into his eyes. He found his grey van, the paint peeling. He sat with his head on the steering wheel. An ache threatened to travel into his heart. Josh sat there until classes let out.

There was something different about Alice and Maria. Even his grandfather didn't seem as grouchy and miserable as he used to. Josh wanted whatever they had. He wanted happiness and not the fleeting delusion of happiness that drugs and alcohol, girls and parties brought. Josh wanted something more.

Chapter 6

Josh stopped by his grandfather's room. The older man held a thick black book in his hand. Its pages crinkled as he turned them. A short plump woman with salt and peppered brown hair sat angrily across from him. There was a dull ache in his heart.

Josh grimaced. "Mom."

"Hello, Love." She smiled at him. It didn't seem as nosy and condescending as usual, but he couldn't help feeling angry. Why was she acting like this after all this time? "What are you doing here?"

His irritation flared. Before he could answer, his grandfather intervened. "He's visiting the little girl next door."

Her eyebrows shot up into her bangs. "You are?"

"No, I'm here because of the food." The sarcasm got him a fiery glare.

His grandfather shooed him out. Marie stood in front of the door to Alice's room. She whispered anxiously into a phone. Her eyes brightened when she saw him. The same way Alice's did. With a relieved slump to her shoulders, she ushered him into the room.

It was cold. The windows were closed and he was overwhelmed by the beeping of machines and quiet sobs. Alice laid with her back towards the door. Her whole body trembled.

Pain gripped at his heart. Josh sat on the edge of her bed. She didn't turn over. He opened his phone, scrolling through *Instagram*. He reclined on the bed.

The sobbing quieted and she curled up next to him. She slung a bony arm across his waist. He cringed at the thought of snot on his favorite jeans but shifted closer instead.

"What's the matter?" he asked.

"I'm scared." Her voice trembled with each word.

Josh put his phone away and placed a sympathetic arm on her tiny back. "Of what?"

She looked up, more tears streamed down her eyes. "Is it going to hurt even more when I die? It already hurts so much."

His voice caught in his throat. Swallowing the lump in his throat, Josh didn't know what to say or if he should say anything at all.

Alice rested her head in the crook in his arm. "What if I can't breathe? My chest feels like it's exploding."

Josh rubbed her beanie. "I don't know. I've never died. I can't imagine your god would be so cruel."

She sat up to hug him. Josh hesitated before gently wrapping his arms around the child. His eyes watered as she sniffled in his shoulder.

"Will you be my brother?" Her voice was so quiet that he barely heard her speak.

He let some tears fall. "I'd love to." His voice cracked.

Marie opened the door as Josh and Alice cried together. She worriedly questioned them. Josh smiled, the first real smile in a long time. Marie finally relaxed while Alice fell asleep. Josh wiped the tears off her cheeks. Marie cuddled on the hospital bed while Josh sat on a chair. He gathered a few of his things, preparing to go.

"Thank you for talking to Alice. I know her chemo treatment makes her act younger than she is." Marie gave him a grin, just like Alice's. "We've been really blessed to have you in our lives."

Josh blushed and rubbed the back of his neck.

"I'm the one who's been— blessed."

Josh walked into his grandfather's room. A bag of personal items was neatly placed on the bed. His grandfather watched their small town through his window. The expression on his grandfather's face was solemn, almost grim. Josh struggled to read it. Josh wondered what was going through his grandfather's mind.

"Want me to drive you home?" Josh asked, causing the older gentleman to whip around faster than he should've.

His grandfather's mouth gaped though he quickly regained his composure. "If you wish."

Josh grabbed his grandfather's stuff. "Wait at the front and I'll bring my car around."

He walked out of the hospital. The warm air brushed against his skin. He practically purred as the fresh air of his little town tickled his nose and ruffled his hair.

Not paying attention to his surroundings, he barreled right into someone.

"I'm sorry." He grabbed their arms and stabilized them. Recognition sunk in. "I didn't mean to, Mom."

She flattened her lips to her face. "Joshua Benjamin Willoughberg, you need to watch where you're going. What if you ran into an elderly—"

Joshua tuned her out. "I've got to get my car, Mom. I'm taking Grandpa home."

Her face turned bright red. "You better not be brushing me off. Where are you going? I am still talking to you."

"Sorry, Mom. I see Grandpa."

She yelled at him as he jogged to the parking garage. He felt bad for leaving her, but Josh didn't want Grandpa to wait too long. He wondered when he last felt bad for ignoring her.

Pulling into the pickup area, Josh saw his mom and grandpa arguing once again. People gave them glares and side eyes.

Josh rolled down the window of his old van. "Do you need a ride too, Mom?"

She swirled her angry expression towards him. It took her a minute to process what he said. His mom's eyes brightened. "I would, thank you."

"It's probably best for Grandpa to sit in the passenger seat."

With a groan, Grandpa settled into his seat. He closed his eyes and gave Josh's mom the silent treatment which she reciprocated.

They lived on the complete opposite sides of town, but it only took ten minutes to drop both of them off at their respective homes. Josh took his mom home first. He didn't want to deal with her for too long.

As his grandfather got out, he chastised Josh. "Your mother isn't a bad person. You need to stop treating her like a villain."

Josh blinked. His brain wrapped around what his grandfather said. "I don't treat her like a villain. She's the one who—"

His grandfather slammed the door shut, and Josh rolled his eyes. What would his grandfather know?

Chapter 7

The sight of Eric standing in front of Joshua's house did not give him warm fuzzy feelings. Josh considered driving around the block until his friend left, but the malicious expression Eric pointed towards the window convinced him otherwise.

Josh pulled into the driveway. Dead grass framed the yard, while a little tree without any leaves reached longingly towards the sun. Brown walls with peeling paint held up a tile roof which needed repairs desperately. He just replaced the windows.

He pasted on his signature smile before stepping out of the car. "Eric? What are you doing here?"

Eric stalked up to him and invaded his personal space. "What was your problem this morning? Were you jealous about Amy? I'll let you have a go at her if you want," he said with a smirk. "She's pretty fun. I think you'd like her."

Josh sighed and said something he never knew he could say, "That wasn't it, but I'm sorry. I shouldn't have said what I did."

Eric frowned, brows furrowing. "What's happened to you?"

Josh shrugged. A beam of light hit his eyes. He shook his head and turned towards it. Scanning the street, nothing shone on the asphalt. His indifferent eyes landed on Eric.

"You don't know?" Eric growled. "Well, I don't like it. We should get a drink and you'll be back to normal."

Josh patted Eric's shoulder. "Thanks for the offer, but I'm not interested. I have some stuff I need to do."

Eric gaped at him before storming off. Josh waved at his back, not really knowing what else to do. He opened the creaky door to his house and was shocked to discover that it was still really clean.

Josh meant to work on homework. He really did. Somehow between assignments, he found himself scrolling through that one famous online shop. In his cart, Josh had three different stuffed animals and a few baby dolls.

As he brought himself back to his homework, the doorbell rang. He slipped off the couch and ran to the door. Mumbling under his breath about interruptions, he peeked through the peephole.

"Can I help you, Amy?" he asked, leaning against the door frame.

Her hair fell over her shoulder. Josh kept his eyes up, feeling guilty about accidentally gazing at her unbuttoned shirt. Red lipstick stained her front tooth as she grinned at him. His heart beat rapidly in his chest. He cursed his unruly emotions.

"I'm sorry about those texts. A friend of mine had my phone." She batted her thick eyelashes. Amy pressed her chest against him. His cheeks flushed. "If you want we could." He followed her line of sight to the inside of the house.

Josh hesitated. Her hands rested her on his chest, sliding up to his neck. She ran her fingers through his hair. He wanted to take her into his arms, this figure of beauty. Her beautiful eyes and body allured him. This was why he wanted her. Sick little Alice popped into his mind, the guilt of disappointing her, and how if she were his age she'd scold him for sleeping around.

Josh pushed her away from his body. "I really, really like you, Amy, but I can't."

She frowned. "Eric's right. Something's definitely wrong with you."

A red sports car passed by. Amy flipped her hair as it made a u-turn and pulled up in his driveaway. This was the most people who had visited his house since he moved in.

"You were better when you were easy." She ran up to the car. She chatted the driver up and offered her goods. The driver let her in.

For a moment, Josh regretted not letting her in. He wanted to feel her, to know her, to be with her. It wasn't like she'd be the first girl he had slept with. Amy was more beautiful than any other girl he knew, so why did he feel so different?

Chapter 8

Josh's grandfather, Jack, never really got those smarty-pants phones. It took him a good thirty minutes to figure out how to get the new fangled taxi service. The person drove up in their own personal car. The driver graciously opened the grey car door for him.

"The name's Henry," the driver said. He brushed his blond hair from his hazel eyes. His flat lips curved into a friendly smile. "Who're you visiting?"

Jack buckled the seatbelt. "My wife."

Henry nodded. He pulled the car out of the driveway. "How long had you been married?"

Jack gave a wry smile. "Fifty years."

Henry whistled in admiration. They neared the cemetery. It was close to his house so he could visit her, but as he got older, it became harder to walk over.

Trees lined the perimeter. They pulled up to the sidewalk and Jack unbuckled himself, readying for his visit.

"Do you have any advice for newlyweds?" Henry rubbed the back of his neck.

Jack leaned back into the car seat. "Keep God centered in your life."

Henry's eyes widened. "God?"

Jack smiled at the young man's disbelief. "It sounds like a ploy, right? My children didn't follow my advice, and they don't go to church at all. However, my grandson is changing. I think the Lord is working in his heart."

Henry paled, obviously uncomfortable. Jack laughed, a deep, raspy sound that rumbled in his chest. "Thanks for listening to an old man ramble."

Jack got out of the small car. Henry rolled down his window and thanked him for the advice. Warm wind dulled his aches and pains as Jack walked through the cemetery. Young couples strolled up to their parents and other loved ones' resting places.

Jack stumbled over the path. He pulled off to a less visited path. Few people walked around him. The solemn air suffocated any emotion. Overgrown trees and weeds overcame the walkway. In a deserted plot laid his wife. He placed a small lamb stuffed animal on the stone, a tradition he had started when they first met. Every year on birthdays and anniversaries, Jack would give her a new stuffed animal. Just because she was gone doesn't mean he'd stop.

He knew she wasn't there in the ground, but he hoped his voice would carry to her. "Ella, I hope you can see our family. Josh is changing. I know he's the one you worried about most."

Jack stayed until the sky turned red and pink. The air cooled and he didn't know who to call. It would take too long to call a taxi.

"Grandpa?" an inquisitive voice called to him.

Jack swiveled. Josh walked up to him, flowers in his arms. He laid carnations on the grave next to the stuffed animal. Jack doubted Josh had ever visited since the funeral. That was years before, back when Josh still attended middle school.

"Do you need another ride?" Josh's eyes twinkled. He was livelier than Jack had seen in years. He laughed when Jack nodded. "You got to get a new ride. What if I move?"

Jack pretended to be grouchy which made Josh laugh more.

"You can't fake it," Josh said.

Oh, how his grandson had changed. Pride swelled in the older man's heart. The angry young man was beginning to cool down. Jack couldn't believe how much the boy had changed in a matter of days. There was hope in Josh's face, a spring in his step, and Jack could barely hold back his grin.

Chapter 9

Alice sat alone once again. Mama left to go eat with Mr. Fiskar. Alice didn't mind too much. Mama kept nagging her and not allowing her to have some fun. Mama needed a break from Alice.

Alice wished someone would open the window. Mama doesn't think she is well enough to have it open though. The pollen in the air could cause harm, or so Mama said. Allie didn't believe that, but she got scolded when she said so. Alice wanted the warm breeze and flowery scent, the warmth of the sun on her skin. She couldn't remember the last time she went outside.

"Boo!"

She squealed and spun around. Josh laughed before turning grim. His pretty features scrunched up in disappointment with himself. Mama made that face all the time.

"Sorry, Allie. I shouldn't have scared you."

Allie hugged him as he sat on the edge of her bed. He hid something behind his back. She tried to peek at whatever it was. He grinned before pulling out a brand new lion. Alice gaped before squeezing Josh as hard as she possibly could, burying her head in his shoulder.

He grabbed her old lion and threw the arm of the new lion on top of it. "I didn't want you or your lion to get too lonely."

She snatched them from him and hugged the two to her chest. "Thank you, Josh!"

Allie invited him to sit with her. Mama came back into the room briefly to check on her while they watched a movie. Mama ruffled his hair and kissed Alice's cheek. Josh's eyes widened from Mama's display of gratitude, but he embraced her affection. Allie snuggled closer to him.

Halfway through the film, while Josh dozed off, Allie cried. She wanted her mom, but she was busy with Mr. Fiskar and work. Josh turned towards her, eyes barely open. He patted her back as she cried.

"I want my mom."

"I'll call her." He pulled out his phone.

Alice shook her head fervently. "I don't want her to hate me."

Josh gazed out the window. His face contorted in pain, but Alice couldn't figure out why. Something caught his eye, but when Alice looked, nothing was there.

"Your mom would never hate you," he finally said with certainty.

"How would you know?"

He tapped his chin, pretending to be thinking. "Well, she obviously loves you a lot. You're her precious kid. She loves you more than anything."

Alice giggled, slightly uplifted. "No, she loves Jesus more."

"Obviously."

Allie turned to the television. "If I was going to grow up, I'd want to marry someone like you. Are you going to get married?"

Josh shook his head. Allie noticed tears welling in his eyes.

"There's this really pretty girl at my church. Her name's Rebekah," Alice explained while nodding. "I think she'd like you."

The door swung open. Alice looked around Josh curiously. Mama walked in with Mr. Fiskar. She happily hung onto his arm. Her smile made Alice angry. Mr.

Fiskar took her Mama away again. Josh got up, taking his comforting presence away, and Alice finally had enough. She cried.

Her cries startled everyone. Mama ran to her side and Josh crouched on the floor. Mr. Fiskar trotted over, but Alice cried louder and harder. Josh looked behind him and took Mr. Fiskar out of the room.

"Baby, what's wrong? Does it hurt?" Mama asked.

"You're leaving me," Alice said, barely understandable in her whiny voice.

Mama wrapped her arms around Alice. She tried to calm her, but it only made Alice more angry. Mama let Alice cry until she stopped because of exhaustion.

Mama laid next to her on the hospital bed. "I'm not leaving you."

Alice pushed her away. "Yes you are. If Mr. Fiskar wasn't around, you'd spend more time with me."

"My little treasure, I'm always here."

Alice shook her head. "You just want me to die so that you can get married!" she yelled. Her face was red and splotchy.

Mama winced. She hugged Alice, though Alice fought with all her might. "I would never wish that. You're my child of old age just like Sarah."

Alice stopped fighting. "You're not a hundred."

"No, but Mama was older when she had you. Logan is not going to get in the way of me and my precious baby."

Alice glanced up at her mama, suspicion written on her face. "Are you sure?"

"Absolutely."

Allie gave her mama a huge hug. Josh peeked his head in to say goodbye. Allie giggled when he hit his head on the door frame.

Chapter 10

Alice cuddled with her raggedy stuffed animal. Tears stained her pillowcase. Her lips split and felt as dry as the desert. She slapped them together, but it only hurt. Everything hurt. Every time she coughed, liquid would travel up her throat, sending burns up it. She hadn't had solid food for who knows how long. Her stomach rumbled, and the craving for macaroni and cheese intensified.

Flipping over sent aches and pains up and down her little broken body. She tried to suck in her breath but choked on more liquid. No matter how much liquid they pumped out, more would fill in its place. Her body spasmed and she let out a cry.

"Can I get you anything, Baby?" her mom asked. Worry creased her forehead.

Alice shook her head. Black crept into her vision and she tried curling into herself. It felt like a bomb was ticking in her head. Each heartbeat caused a headache to throb. Her nausea turned to vomit.

As if her dry heaving was a sign, Alice knew her body was shutting down. The pain wrecked her body. Her mom called her name, but even if she wanted to respond, she couldn't. With each convulsion, her mind let go. The breathing tube took complete control of her lungs. Tears pooled out of her blue eyes. "Mommy."

For a moment, the pain stopped. The next, it was so extreme that her consciousness slipped.

* * *

Josh walked in at the worst moment. The room buzzed with chaos. Josh couldn't even enter as nurses ran around. Marie hung onto Alice's hands for dear life. Nurse Polis shook his head grimly. The medical staff left the room. Josh walked in. His heart felt like it was going to explode.

"They said she doesn't have much time," Marie whispered. "I knew she wasn't going to. At first, they told us it wasn't that bad."

Josh pulled up a chair next to Marie, sagging into it.

"Most kids survive Leukemia. They told me she'd make it!"

Josh held Alice's hand and warmed her frigid fingers. The beeping of the heart monitor echoed in his head. Over and over again, he concentrated on the steady pulse. It wasn't strong but each heartbeat was there, keeping the young girl alive. Marie buried her head in her hands. Sobs melted into the beeping of the equipment.

"Marie," a deep bass spoke behind them.

She jumped up and ran to the speaker. He was a tall man with a potbelly. His balding head reflected with the fluorescent light. "Logan!" They hugged. "Josh, this is my fiance, Logan. Logan, this is Josh. I told you about him the other day."

Josh reluctantly let go of Allie's hand. She shifted slightly. Her eyes fluttered open for a split second. He wanted to watch over her in case she woke, but he greeted Logan. Logan wrapped Josh up in a warm and friendly hug. Josh stiffened before letting himself sag into the hug.

Josh sat back down and petted Alice's beanie. "Allie, as your older brother I cannot condone this behavior." His voice trembled. "So you have to wake up, okay? You got to wake up."

Marie rested a hand on Josh's shoulder. He stood up, wiped his eyes, and left. He couldn't stay there any longer. A piece of his heart felt as if it was dying

alongside that little child.

Chapter 11

Josh shocked himself when he got home. He called his mom and not because he needed cash. He didn't know who else to call, who would listen, who would understand. There was no way Eric and him were still friends. He didn't have anyone else. Relief flooded his senses when she answered. She sounded worried and sad.

"Did something happen? Is there a baby? Do you need money?" His mom poured out question after question.

He laughed sadly. "No, Mom."

There was silence. The AC kicked on, filling the empty room.

"Mom, are you still there?"

"I'm— I'm sorry. I was taken by surprise. I think this is the first time you've called me not asking for money. What happened?"

Josh leaned into his sofa, head resting in between the cushions. His voice wavered and he couldn't bring himself to talk. He sniffled. He couldn't understand why a little girl made such an impact on his life. She was small and childish, but Alice cheered him up and wanted him to be better. He wanted to be someone that she'd be proud of.

His mom understood his silence. "It's that little girl, right?"

"She's dying. Every time I see her, a little bit more is gone. Her arms are so bony, and the oxygen tank thing is in complete control of her breathing." He took a deep shaking breath. "I wonder why I didn't meet that family sooner. It's a small town and they stick out like a sore thumb. How did I miss them?"

"It might not have been the time before. Would you have acknowledged them a month ago?" In the background, he heard his mom's car engine rev. "I'm on my way." He would never admit it to her but he was happy that she still wanted to come over.

Ten minutes later, his mom sat on the couch in his living room. She brought hot cocoa and a movie with popcorn. It was the first conversation since he was a child, maybe since middle school, that neither of them screamed at each other. For the first time in a long time, Josh felt only love and respect for the woman who gave him life. And he sympathized with her. Not that he had any children, that he was aware of that is, but he began to understand what she was feeling.

"Your house is cleaner than I expected." Her tone irritated him a little, but he kept his mouth shut.

Josh and his mom talked about many things. For several hours, Josh took the time to understand his mom and he felt like his mom had taken time to understand him. They did argue, but Josh apologized quickly. Another first in a long time or maybe ever. Apologizing had been so hard for him. Even then, it took everything he had to swallow his pride and apologize. He had more to apologize for, so much more. His mom patiently waited for him to find the right words.

"I forgive you."

He tried to judge her expression. "Are you sure? Why so easily? I've fought you on everything. I ignored all your advice. Why would you forgive me?"

She gave him a small smile. "I am your mother, Joshua. I love you more than anything on this planet. You will always be my little boy. That is why I forgive you, because I love you."

Chapter 12

Josh pulled on a coat as fast as he could. Running out of his tiny house, he barely remembered to lock the door. He didn't care though. Marie was on the phone, telling him it was time. He ran. Sweat ran down his forehead. Alice could pass away at any moment. He prayed for the first time in his life. With all of his heart, he prayed that God would let him see her one last time.

"I beg of you, if you're real God, let me see her one last time." His voice cracked.

Josh whipped his car out of the parking lot. Cars honked at him, but no lights turned red as he drove. No traffic stopped in front of him. He made it to the hospital in record time. His heart raced. He worried that they would have to admit him for weird heart palpitations.

The hospital felt colder than usual. Despite his coat, he couldn't stop shivering. It was practically silent besides the beeping of heart monitors. Nurses rushed to and fro in a more solemn manner than what he was used to. He checked in and got his wrist band. He tapped his foot impatiently. It felt like time had slowed down.

Nurse Polis recognized him immediately and ushered him into Alice's room. Her mother cried next to her sleeping body. His grandfather was there, standing off to the side. Jack's shoulders slumped in defeat. Logan Fiskar rested a hand on Marie's shaking body. Josh went to the other side of the hospital bed.

Alice's cheeks were gaunt. She couldn't breathe on her own and each shuddering breath broke his heart. Her face contracted in pain and sweat and tears dripped down her cheek. In a matter of moments, God would take her home and Josh cried. He didn't bother trying to hide it. He grabbed her warm hand.

"Mommy," she said. Each breath took great effort.

"I'm here, treasure."

Alice smiled. Tears fell from her eyes. "I love you, Mommy."

Marie sobbed louder. "I love you too. I love you so much, my little treasure."

Alice coughed. It was wet and raspy. Josh tried to stop his own tears, but couldn't. Her heart rate slowed. Her breathing was fully regulated by a machine. She whimpered. Her blue eyes were clouded, unfocused. It was all the child could do to keep her eyes open.

"Josh," Alice whispered, though Josh knew she would've spoken louder if she could. His heart warmed slightly that she would call to him despite her pain. "I'll miss you."

"Aren't you going to Jesus? You'll have no time to think of me." His voice shook. Her blue eyes grew tired and her eyelids slowly closed. Her knees shot to her chest.

"It hurts." Alice squeezed his hand and sobbed. Snot ran down her nose and onto her lip. "I don't want to die yet."

Marie let out a cry. Josh bit his lip so that he wouldn't make any distressing sounds. The heart monitor slowed.

"I know." Josh kissed her forehead and smiled. "Will you wait for me?"

Her heart rate was at emergency level, but the doctors could do no more. Her eyes fluttered shut. The beep of her heart stopping filled the room. Her hand was warm though. Alice was gone before she could answer. Why did she have to go?

"My treasure," Marie cried in anguish, holding her baby against her. She rocked back and forth.

Grandfather wiped his eyes and hugged Marie. She sobbed on his shoulder. The room filled with heart wrenching screaming.

"My baby." Her voice quieted.

A precious soul went to heaven, leaving broken hearts on earth. Josh left the room. He didn't want to be in there any longer. He admired the child's strength even in death. Josh wished he could've done more, done anything.

His grandfather sat next to him. "Death comes for all of us especially when we least expect it."

"But we expected it! We couldn't even do something to ease her suffering." Josh contained his voice in a harsh whisper.

His grandfather sighed. They watched her bed be wheeled away. Each step the cornorers took created a sad rift in his heart. His grandfather patted his back. He looked less grumpy than usual, but in place of his grumpiness was a sorrowful wisdom that cut deep.

Josh opened his mouth to speak, but his grandfather stood up. "I'll stay at your house tonight."

"Okay."

Even though neither of them spoke on the way home, Josh enjoyed their time together. Their grief bonded them. Alice helped him fix so much in his life. Nothing was perfect and it never would be, but his new mindset created new opportunities.

Three days later, Josh received a phone call from Marie. The funeral was scheduled and they wanted him to speak at it. Josh cried over the phone.

Chapter 13

The church was tiny, but bursting at the seams with people. All of them donned black or navy blue. Tears streamed down many faces. Josh's own face felt puffy. Marie hugged him as he passed by. Her thanks rang empty against his ears. Josh was an emotional wreck.

"God has a weird sense of humor," Josh said under his breath.

His mother's eyebrows knitted together. "God? I didn't know you believed in a deity."

Josh gave a sad smile. "I didn't. Not until last week at least."

His mom wrinkled her thick brow.

"At my lowest point, He sent me to a child who believed in everything He stood for " Josh laughed sadly and buried his head in his hands.

His mom chuckled. "You definitely aren't a fan of children."

"She was different though. I wanted to be her big brother, to keep her from what she was going through, to keep her safe." Josh leaned against his mom's shoulder. "She was so young. She could've done so much."

His mom rocked him back and forth as he sobbed. "I think she did."

A man in a fancy black suit led the crowd in beautiful, powerful hymns; hymns about being freed from sin, of having a friend in Jesus, and of going to Heaven. Joshua was jealous of their hope and conviction, of their freedom and joy, of how despite being so sad, they knew they'd see her again. Josh wanted that.

Once the song leader moved, Josh stood up. Awkwardly, he made his way in front of the crowd. They looked up at him with expectation. He didn't feel nervous though. Josh knew that they were with him in his opinions of Alice.

He cleared his throat. "I'm Josh. Actually, I'm one of the souls that was affected by Alice. I met her by accident or fate or God's intervention. Alice had a horrible personality. She just went with the flow of things and made everyone else follow her lead. It was so rude of her." A few people laughed.

"Without her, I would be drunk at a bar or trying to hook up with whoever at school. I gained a younger sibling who I loved dearly. I wish I had met her earlier. I never would've believed in God without her faith. I just wish I knew I'd see her again when I die."

Josh thanked everyone for listening and went back to his mom. She ruffled his hair. A young woman about his age sang. Her auburn hair curled nicely at the ends and her voice sounded like an angel. The song brought tears to his eyes.

"Thank you, Rebekah, for singing Alice's favorite hymn," Marie said. "She always loved your voice."

Rebekah wiped at her eyes. "She meant a lot to me."

An older gentleman, about fifty years old, came up and preached. Josh didn't comprehend a thing the man read. The language was too old. When the man started speaking, it was like a fire was lit in Josh's softened heart. Ephesians chapter 2, verses 8 and 9 were read. " For by grace are ye saved through faith; and that not of yourselves: it is the gift of God: Not of works, lest any man should boast." The sermon was easy to understand. The passion behind the message inspired him and hurt him. Josh wanted this salvation, not the one he had been trying to pursue.

As soon as the service ended, Josh made his way to the front. Alice's body rested in a small casket. They had painted makeup on her face as if she were a painting. It was so fake like badly done plastic surgery. A blonde wig was placed perfectly on her tiny head. Despite the fake face, Josh imagined her getting up and surprising him.

"I'm glad y'all could make it. I'm Pastor Michael Moore." The large preacher firmly shook his hand.

"Josh," he nodded.

Pastor Moore smiled. "I'm sorry that we've gotta meet in such distressing circumstances. Can I help you in any way?"

Josh nodded. "I was wondering if you could tell me more about this God that the Casablanca family believes in."

The pastor's smile deepened, "It would be my pleasure."

Epilogue

"Daddy," his daughter called. Her lopsided smile had a few teeth missing. She stumbled as she transitioned from school bus to sidewalk.

Josh gathered her up into his arms, smiling. "How was school, my sweet girl?"

She laughed as he gave her a kiss on the cheek, scruffy beard tickling her face. Her brown pigtails bounced as he walked up their driveway. "My friend Megan said her mom want to come to church with us."

"That's awesome."

"Josh, Alice, hurry inside. I actually made cookies that didn't turn out oily," Rebekah yelled from the front door of their house.

His little girl wiggled out of his arms and ran to her mother. Josh couldn't contain his joy. Everything wasn't perfect and would never be in this sin cursed world, but meeting Alice in the hospital changed the course of his life. He met Rebekah, his beautiful bride, at Allie and Marie's home church, and they were about to have their second child. God had gotten his life together. If he were to die that moment, he knew for certain Jesus and Allie would be waiting for him.

"Dad, Grandma and Grandpa are on their way." Alice hopped up and down in front of the doorway. "Also, Nana Marie said she'd stop by too."

"We'd better finish cleaning, shouldn't we?" He gave her a side eye.

She gulped and her chocolate brown eyes widened. Screaming, she ran back into the house. Josh hoped it was to clean her room. There wasn't even a pathway to her bed from the door. Rebekah grew more upset with each passing day. He might need to get on to Alice.

A blinding light reflected into his eye. Josh turned towards the sky. It was pleasantly warm and the rich smell of rain began to roll in with the clouds. A bit of sun peeked through the clouds in a stream of light as if heaven was pointing to a particular place on earth. Allie would've loved it.

Josh walked into his lovely home. On the table by the door alongside his car keys, there were two lion stuffed animals. One was falling apart at the seams and had seen better days. The other one was aging, but definitely not as well loved as the first. He rubbed the head of the older one. Rebekah kissed his cheek as he walked into the squeaky clean kitchen.

Josh rested his hand on her baby bump. Their son kicked and Josh kissed Rebekah's stomach. They'd already decided on his name. Jack would grow to be a great man if he was anything like his great grandfather.

Each day with his family was a treasure and he would never forget that, never take it for granted.

Oh, death is an equalizer, all right. No one can escape it. It still comes for the young, the old, the rich, the poor. No matter how good or bad you are: death will come for you. After all, death is inevitable. But he knew that death wasn't the end. It didn't have to be endless suffering either. Death had been conquered. Joshua knew this now. Isn't it amazing how one life changes everything?

Acknowledgements

First of all, I want to praise the Lord for all that He's done for me. I wouldn't be here without Him. His grace and mercy are my hope and peace. I would have never gotten this story without His impact in my life. If you don't know Him, I highly suggest that you do. God is the worker of miracles and the giver of everlasting peace. He is my purpose and my identity, and I hope that maybe one day He'll be yours as well.

I also want to thank my parents and sister. I love you guys so much. Your support of my dreams and unconditional love, despite me being a ginormous turd burglar, is honestly amazing. Because of you guys, I didn't have to hide my passions. Though, Naomi, I can simp for whoever I want. They don't exist so it's fine. Thanks Nomes for utterly demolishing me and my story during editing. It hurt, but this one time you were right. I hope I make you proud. God has truly blessed me.

A special thanks to the pastors' wives that have made such an impact on my life and the lives of my loved ones. You guys are wonderful and I can never thank you enough for your guidance, friendship, and love. There is little I wouldn't do for you and your families. I hope the Lord continues to use you in the lives of others, just as He did for me.

To my lovely creative writing girls, you were a blast to have class with. Your support, both with this and with everything else, has meant the world to me. Thank you for reading this when it was in that "what the heck is going on stage". I love you all so very much. Wherever you go, I pray the Lord will bless you.

I want to thank the awesome ladies I met through my bookstagram. Shannon, you were one of my first friends there. Getting to know you and being able to read your work has been such a pleasure. I will forever simp

for Linus. Ruby, you are legit an angel. Thank you so

much for designing the cover. I can't wait until your book

comes out. There are so many of you that I look up to and

wish I could acknowledge, but I have to pay for each

page. Once I get WYRIA finished, I'll thank more of you

wonderful humans. Plus without Kara, this would be a hot

mess because I suck at grammar.

Finally, I want to thank YOU. First of all, I'm

impressed you've read this far. I usually skip the

acknowledgements, but good for you. Second, you read

my writing. That means more than words could ever

express. I'm pleased and embarrassed. Pleased because

you were actually interested enough in my summary,

cover, or Instagram to pick this up. I'm embarrassed that

you picked this up and read it. I promise, I don't need

therapy. I hope that you enjoyed it and that you'll

remember it. You are loved by God. No matter who you are or what you've done will cause Him not to love you. If you don't know Jesus as your personal savior, I can tell you from personal experience that you're missing out. My most earnest and most heartfelt desire is that you come to know Christ. Thank you so much for reading this.

About the Author

From a young age, Lorelei R. Jensen has adored books. Reading with a flashlight late into the night wasn't uncommon for her at all. She wrote off and on during elementary school, but it wasn't until she got hold of her first self-published book that she decided she wanted to be an author. Currently, she lives with her parents and younger sister in the hot and dry desert of Arizona.

Instagram: @reading_instead_of_sleeping